For Great Aunt Mags, as funky as Mrs Muffly -
much loved, and greatly missed

First published in Great Britain and in the USA in 2008 by
Frances Lincoln Children's Books, 4 Torriano Mews,
Torriano Avenue, London NW5 2RZ
www.franceslincoln.com

British Library Cataloguing in Publication Data available on request

ISBN 978-1-84507-761-7

Illustrated with mixed media

Set in Stone Sans and handlettering

Printed in China

2 4 6 8 9 7 5 3 1

Mrs Muffly's

Monster

Sarah Dyer

F

FRANCES LINCOLN
CHILDREN'S BOOKS

Mrs Muffly lives in a house on top of a hill.
She has always been a bit strange, but lately
she has been acting very, very strangely indeed.
We think that's because she is keeping
a HUGE monster in her house!

This MUST be true because
on Monday
Mrs Muffly went out and
bought a great big pile of sugar.

We think that's because she needs lots of sugar to sweeten him up...

and make him much less scary.

On Tuesday
Mrs Muffly went out and
bought 27 dozen eggs.

We think
that's because
the monster
needs a lot of
eggs to
style his hair
in the morning.

On Wednesday
Mrs Muffly went out and
bought 58 packs of butter.

We think that's because the monster
has the roughest feet in the world.
He needs the butter to soften them up.

On Thursday
Mrs Muffly
went out
and bought
41 sacks
of flour.

We think that's because the monster
uses them as pillows to sleep on at night.
(He's a fussy monster.)

On Friday
Mrs Muffly went out and
bought 464 jars of jam.

We think that's because the monster
loves having really deep jam baths.

On Saturday

Mrs Muffly didn't come out at all.

All that could be seen from her house on the hill

were enormous clouds of smoke, flames

and scary shapes at the windows.

We think the monster must have escaped

and eaten poor Mrs Muffly!

On Sunday it was the Giant Cake Competition. And there, right in the middle of all the cakes, was Mrs Muffly (with not the slightest sign of being eaten) with first prize for the biggest... MONSTER-SIZED CAKE EVER!

BUT we think
she must have had
some help!

Recipe for a not-quite-so-monster-sized cake

Ingredients

110 g/4 oz/½ cup butter or margarine

110 g/4 oz/½ cup caster or superfine sugar

2 medium eggs

110 g/4 oz/ 1 cup self-raising flour

Strawberry jam

Method

1. Heat the oven to 180 C/350 F/Gas 4.

2. Line two 18 cm/7 inch cake tins with baking parchment.

3. Use a hand mixer to cream the butter and the sugar together until pale and fluffy.

4. Beat in the eggs, one by one.

5. Sift the flour and fold in using a large metal spoon.

6. Divide the mixture between the cake tins and gently spread out with a spatula.

7. Bake for 20-25 minutes until golden brown and firm to the touch.

8. Allow the cakes to stand for 5 minutes before turning out on to a wire rack to cool.

9. Sandwich the cakes together with the jam.